HOLD TIGHT!

To Anne McNeil

HOLD TIGHT!
A RED FOX BOOK 978 1 862 30649 3

First published in Great Britain by The Bodley Head,
an imprint of Random House Children's Books

The Bodley Head edition published 2002
Red Fox edition published 2003

3 5 7 9 10 8 6 4 2

Red Fox Books are published by Random House Children's Books,
61–63 Uxbridge Road, London W5 5SA,
a division of The Random House Group Ltd,
in Australia by Random House Australia (Pty) Ltd,
20 Alfred Street, Milsons Point, Sydney, NSW 2061, Australia,
in New Zealand by Random House New Zealand Ltd,
18 Poland Road, Glenfield, Auckland 10, New Zealand,
and in South Africa by Random House (Pty) Ltd,
Endulini, 5A Jubilee Road, Parktown 2193, South Africa

THE RANDOM HOUSE GROUP Limited Reg. No. 954009
www.**kids**at**randomhouse**.co.uk

A CIP catalogue record for this book is available from the British Library.

Printed in Singapore

HOLD TIGHT!

JOHN PRATER

RED FOX

Grandbear was busy . . .

Baby Bear was
busy, too.

"*Vroom, vroom!* I'm on a plane,"
said Baby Bear. "Want to come?"

"OK. Just a quick
ride then," said
Grandbear.

"HOLD TIGHT!"

"Hip, hooray,
We're on our way,
Flying high and low . . ."

"But now
we're flying
upside down . . ."

"... and over we all go! Now I must do the washing."

But before Grandbear could pick up the washing, Baby Bear scrambled back into the box.

"Now what?" asked Grandbear.
"*Choo-choo! Chuff-chuff!* I'm on a train,"
said Baby Bear. "Want to come?"
"OK. Just a quick ride then,"
said Grandbear.

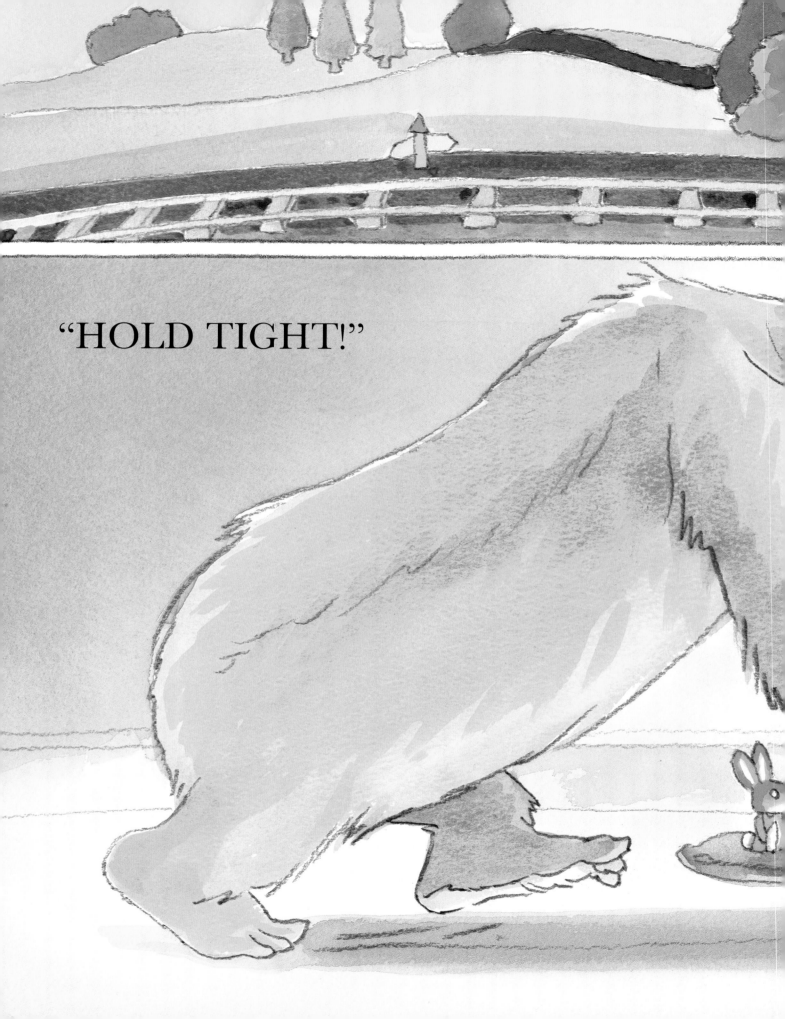

"HOLD TIGHT!"

"Hip, hooray,
We're on our way,
Going very
slow . . ."

"But faster now,
and faster still . . ."

" . . . and over
we all go! Now
I must do the
washing."

But before Grandbear could
pick up the washing basket,
Baby Bear scrambled
into it.

"Now what?"
asked
Grandbear.

"*Splish, splash!* I'm on a boat,"
said Baby Bear. "Want to come?"
Grandbear sighed and said, "OK,
just a very quick ride, but then I
must get on."

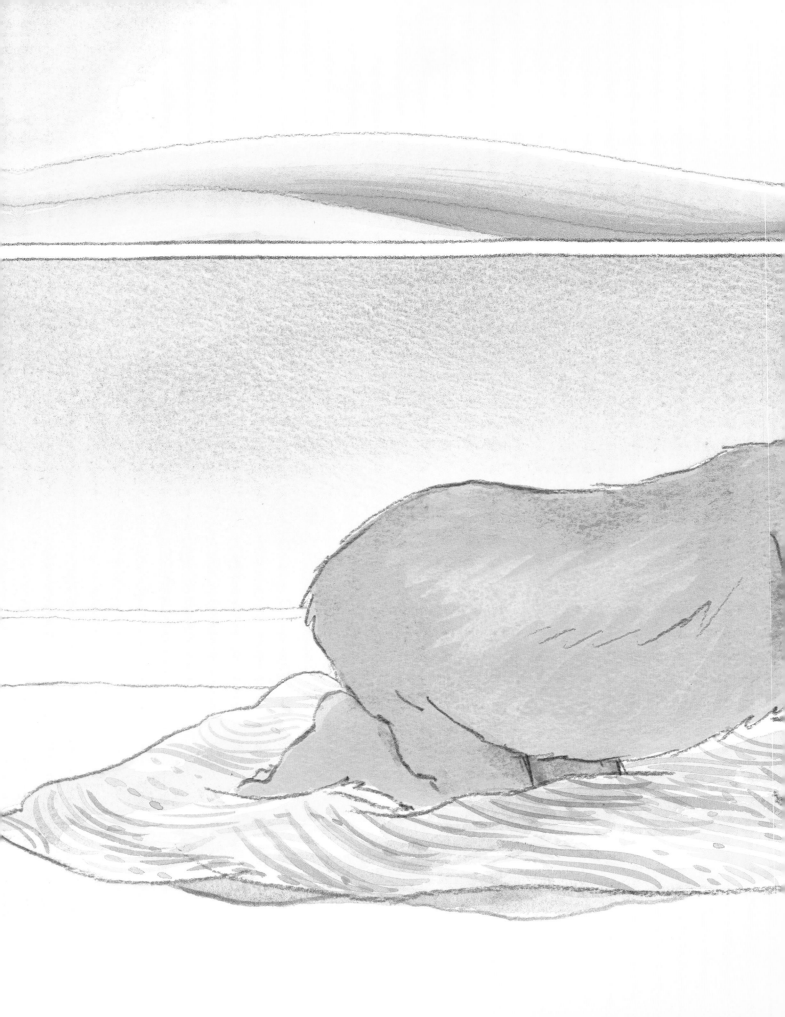

"HOLD TIGHT!"

"Hip, hooray,
We're on our way,
Bobbing to and fro.
But, look!
Here comes a
great big wave . . ."

" . . . and over we all go!"

"Now I really *must*
do the washing,"
said Grandbear.

"OK," said Baby Bear. "Can I come?"

"HOLD TIGHT!"

"Hip, hooray,
We're on our way
To get the washing done.
We've ridden on a plane,
A boat,
A train,
We've had a lot of fun . . ."

". . . and HERE WE ARE!"

"Oh," said Baby Bear.
"Just one more ride.
Pleeease!"

"All right," said Grandbear.
"Just *one* more. And this
will be the very best ride of all."

"HOLD TIGHT!"

Other Baby Bear books to share:

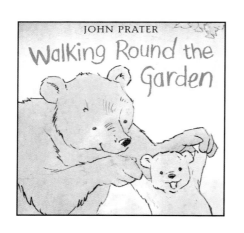

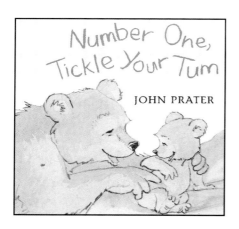